JULIUS
CAESAR

Artist: Li Sidong

First edition for North America (including Canada and Mexico), Philippine Islands, and Puerto Rico published in 2009 by Barron's Educational Series, Inc.

All inquiries should be addressed to:
Barron's Educational Series, Inc.
250 Wireless Blvd.
Hauppauge, NY 11788
www.barronseduc.com

ISBN-13 (Hardcover): 978-0-7641-6141-4
ISBN-10 (Hardcover): 0-7641-6141-5
ISBN-13 (Paperback): 978-0-7641-4010-5
ISBN-10 (Paperback): 0-7641-4010-8

Library of Congress Control No.: 2007906903

Picture credits:
p. 40 Topham Picturepoint/TopFoto.co.uk
p. 42 Topham Picturepoint/TopFoto.co.uk
p. 45 Mark Bergin
p. 47 Topham Picturepoint/Topfoto
Every effort has been made to trace copyright holders. The Salariya Book Company apologizes for any omissions and would be pleased, in such cases, to add an acknowledgment in future editions.

Printed and bound in China.
Printed on paper from sustainable sources.
9 8 7 6 5 4 3 2 1

JULIUS CAESAR

WILLIAM SHAKESPEARE

Illustrated by
Li Sidong

Retold by
Michael Ford

Series created and designed by
David Salariya

Brutus: Gentle friends,
Let's kill him boldly,
but not wrathfully;
Let's carve him as a dish
fit for the gods,
Not hew him as a carcass
fit for hounds.

MAIN CHARACTERS

Brutus,
a senator

Julius Caesar,
consul of Rome

Mark Antony,
a senator

Portia, wife
of Brutus

Calpurnia,
wife of Caesar

Cassius,
a senator

Casca,
a tribune

Cicero, a
senator

Octavius Caesar, nephew
to Julius Caesar

Cinna the poet

Flavius and Marullus,
tribunes

A soothsayer

A HERO'S RETURN?

Rome, 44 BC.

On the Feast of Lupercalia, citizens fill the streets to celebrate Julius Caesar's triumphant return to Rome. Four years ago, Caesar defeated his former friend Pompey the Great in a civil war. Now he has beaten Pompey's sons as well.

The tribunes[1] Marullus and Flavius are trying to make their way through the crowded streets.

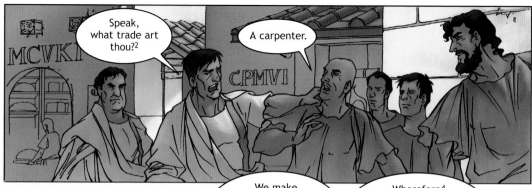

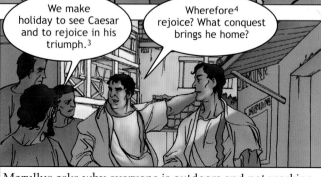

Marullus asks why everyone is outdoors and not working.

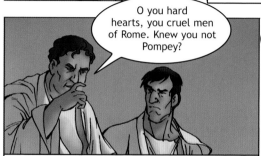

He doesn't think Caesar's return deserves such celebration. The consul[5] Pompey did much more for Rome.

Flavius tells Marullus to try and calm the people, and to take down any decorations they have put up around the city.

1. tribune: a magistrate elected by the people.　2. art thou?: are you?　3. triumph: a grand procession to welcome a returning hero.　4. wherefore: why.　5. consul: the highest position in the Roman Senate.　6. images: statues of Caesar.　7. decked with ceremonies: decorated.

THE BEGINNINGS OF REVOLT

Caesar's procession makes its way through the streets toward the Palatine Hill[1] while the people celebrate.

Forget not in your speed, Antonio, to touch Calpurnia...

The barren,[2] touched in this holy chase,[3] shake off their sterile[4] curse.

Beware the Ides of March![6]

Caesar has no heir, because his wife is sterile. He reminds his general and friend, Mark Antony, of a Roman superstition of how the sterile may become fertile.[5]

A soothsayer[7] calls out to Caesar as he passes.

He is a dreamer, let us leave him.

The man is brought before Caesar, who dismisses his warning.

8

1. Palatine Hill: one of seven small hills on which the city of Rome was built. It is one of the most ancient parts of the city.   2. barren: unable to produce children.
3. holy chase: sacred procession.   4. sterile: means the same as "barren."   5. fertile: able to bear children.
6. Ides of March: the 15th of March.   7. soothsayer: a person who claims to foretell the future.

Once Caesar and his followers have passed by, the senators[1] Cassius and Brutus remain.

Will you go see the order of the course?[2]

I am not gamesome.[3]

I do lack some part of that quick spirit[4] that is in Antony.

If I have veiled my look[5]...

I turn the trouble of my countenance merely upon myself.[6]

Cassius asks Brutus, his brother-in-law, what is the matter.

What means this shouting?

I do fear the people choose Caesar for their king.

Cassius says the people of Rome love Brutus. Brutus is suspicious of his flattery. They hear shouts.

Cassius tests Brutus's loyalty to Caesar. He hopes Brutus will join his plot to get rid of Caesar.

Cassius tells how he once saved Caesar from drowning and how fever turned this "god" into a coward.

Ay, do you fear it?

Then must I think you would not have it so.

Once, upon a raw and gusty day...

...'tis true, this god did shake.

The fault, dear Brutus, is not in our stars...

What you would work me to, I have some aim.[7]

but in ourselves.

He suggests that they are to blame for Caesar's fame.

Casca brings news that Caesar was offered the crown, but refused it.

The common herd was glad.[8]

Well, Brutus, thou art noble...

Yet, I see, thy honorable mettle may be wrought from that it is disposed.[9]

The men arrange to meet the next night, and Cassius is left alone.

1. senators: members of the Senate, the governing body of ancient Rome.   2. the order of the course: the rest of the procession.
3. gamesome: fun-loving.   4. quick spirit: enthusiasm.   5. veiled my look: frowned.   6. I turn . . . myself: I'm thinking about my own problems.   7. What you . . . aim: I know what you're trying to make me do.   8. The common herd was glad: The common folk were cheering (because this act further convinces the people that Caesar is noble).   9. thy honorable . . . disposed: though you are honorable, it is possible to persuade you.

9

OMENS FROM THE HEAVENS

That night, thunder and lightning crash across the city.

Good even,[1] Casca.

Why are you breathless, and why stare you so?

Casca rushes into the street, pale with fear. Cicero spots him.

Either there is a civil strife in heaven[2]...

...or else the world, too saucy[3] with the gods, incenses[4] them to send destruction.

Casca says he has seen many terrifying things tonight. The gods must be angry.

He's seen a slave with his hands on fire, and he met a lion by the Capitol.[5]

Yesterday he heard there were men walking down the streets on fire...

...and an owl had sat screeching in the marketplace in broad daylight.

1. even: evening. 2. civil strife in heaven: war between the gods. 3. saucy: insolent, rude.
4. incenses: angers. 5. Capitol: another of the seven hills of Rome, site of the temple of Jupiter and the ancient citadel.

Indeed, it is a strange-disposed[1] time.

But men may construe things after their fashion, clean from the purpose of the things themselves.[2]

Cicero leaves, and Cassius arrives to meet Casca.

A man no mightier than thyself or me.

'Tis Caesar that you mean.

Cicero thinks Casca is exaggerating.

Cassius says one man is responsible for the anger of the gods. They think Caesar wants to rule alone.

Indeed they say the senators tomorrow mean to establish Caesar as a king.

So every bondman[3] in his own hand bears[4] the power to cancel his captivity.

I know where I will wear this dagger then.

If they don't want to be ruled, Caesar must die.

Cinna the senator arrives. Cassius has already convinced him and other senators to help. They'll be ready to kill Caesar once his friend Brutus is on their side.

O Cassius, if you could but win the noble Brutus to our party.[5]

Take this paper...lay it in the praetor's[6] chair...

...where Brutus may but find it.

Three parts of him is ours already...

...and the man entire, upon the next encounter, yields him ours.

Casca and Cassius will go to Brutus's house to try to persuade him to help them with the plot.

1. strange-disposed: odd.   2. But men . . . themselves: People tend to interpret things in their own way, and may not understand the real meaning at all.   3. bondman: slave.   4. bears: holds.   5. win . . . party: convince Brutus to join us.   6. praetor: senior magistrate—a position in the senate held by Brutus.

BRUTUS, MAN OF THE PEOPLE

Get me a taper[2] in my study, Lucius. When it is lighted, come and call me here.

Meanwhile...

It must be by his death: and, for my part I know no personal cause to spurn at him...

...but for the general.[1]

Brutus cannot sleep, and paces through his orchard, deep in thought.

I found this paper, thus sealed up, and I am sure it did not lie there when I went to bed.

Lucius returns, and shows Brutus a piece of paper he found lying on the floor. It calls him to take action in Rome's name.

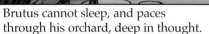

Rome is a Republic,[3] and shouldn't be ruled by one man. Brutus knows he has to kill Caesar.

"Brutus, thou sleep'st. Awake and see thyself...

Speak, strike, redress!"[4]

O Rome, I make thee promise, if the redress will follow,...

...thou receivest thy full petition...

...at the hand of Brutus.

The plotters enter the garden, led by Cassius.

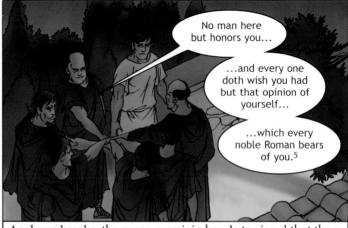

No man here but honors you...

...and every one doth wish you had but that opinion of yourself...

...which every noble Roman bears of you.[5]

As dawn breaks, the seven men join hands to signal that they are all dedicated to the plot.

1. I know . . . general: I have no personal reason to attack him, except for the benefit of the Roman people.
2. taper: candle.   3. Republic: a country that is not led by a monarch, but by elected representatives.
4. redress: rectify a wrong.   5. No man . . . bears of you: Every noble Roman respects you (Brutus), and we all wish you had the same opinion of yourself.

I think it is not meet[1] Mark Antony, so well beloved of Caesar, should outlive Caesar.

Think not of him, for he can do no more than Caesar's arm when Caesar's head is off.

Cassius urges them to kill Mark Antony as well, but Brutus says they should kill only Caesar—otherwise they will seem like criminals.

But it is doubtful yet whether Caesar will come forth today or no.[2]

Never fear that. If he be so resolved,[3] I can o'ersway him.[4]

One of the plotters, Decius, will make sure Caesar comes to the Senate House.

Make me acquainted with[5] your cause of grief.

I am not well in health, and that is all.

Portia, go in awhile.

And by and by[7] thy bosom shall partake the secrets of my heart.

There is a knock at the door.

Brutus's wife, Portia, wants to know why he has been acting strangely. She begs him to tell the truth.

You have some sick offense[6] within your mind, which…I ought to know of.

The senator Ligarius arrives.

I am not sick, if Brutus have in hand[8] any exploit worthy the name of honor.

Such an exploit have I in hand…had you a healthful ear to hear of it.

What it is, my Caius,[9] I shall unfold to thee,[10] as we are going to whom it must be done.[11]

Ligarius seems ill, but says he will feel better if Brutus admits to taking part in the conspiracy.

Ligarius declares that his sickness has left him at hearing this news. Brutus explains the plot.

1. not meet: not right. 2. no: not. 3. if he be so resolved: if that's what he decides. 4. o'ersway him: change his mind. 5. Make me acquainted with: Let me know. 6. sick offense: horrible deed. 7. by and by: soon. 8. have in hand: is planning. 9. Caius: Ligarius's first name. 10. unfold to thee: reveal to you. 11. to whom it must be done: to the person (Caesar) to whom the deed must be done.

CAESAR'S DILEMMA

Nor heaven nor earth have been at peace tonight.

Thrice[1] hath Calpurnia in her sleep cried out, "Help, ho! They murder Caesar!"

Dawn, at Caesar's palace…

Caesar is troubled. His wife Calpurnia slept badly and spoke in her sleep.

Go bid the priests do present sacrifice…

…and bring me their opinions of success.

He tells his servants to ask the priests what the day will hold for him.

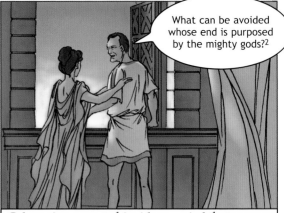

What can be avoided whose end is purposed by the mighty gods?[2]

Calpurnia comes to his side, worried that he is in danger.

Caesar should be a beast without a heart[3] if he should stay at home today for fear.

The beast sacrificed by the priests had no heart. This is a bad omen. Caesar should not go out today, but he is determined.

Alas, my lord, your wisdom is consumed in confidence![4] Do not go forth today.

Calpurnia suggests that Caesar send Mark Antony to the senate in his place.

14

1. Thrice: Three times.   2. What . . . gods?: How can we avoid anything that the gods have decided?
3. without a heart: without courage.   4. your wisdom is consumed in confidence: your bravery is foolish.

For his wife's sake, Caesar agrees.

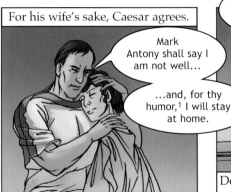

Mark Antony shall say I am not well...

...and, for thy humor,[1] I will stay at home.

I will not come today. Tell them so, Decius.

Most mighty Caesar, let me know some cause.[2]

Calpurnia here, my wife, stays me at home.

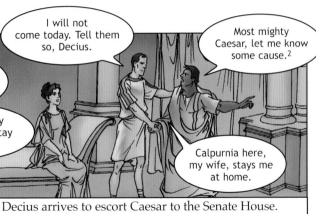

Decius arrives to escort Caesar to the Senate House.

Caesar says Calpurnia dreamed of a statue of him, dripping with blood.

The people dipped their hands into it.

The Senate have concluded to give...

...a crown to mighty Caesar.

Decius suggests another interpretation.

How foolish do your fears seem now, Calpurnia! I am ashamed I did yield to them.[3]

Give me my robe, for I will go.

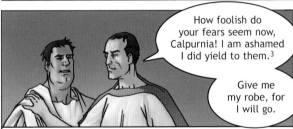

He warns that they might change their minds.

I have an hour's talk in store for you. Remember that you call on me today. Be near me, that I may remember you.[4]

The conspirators arrive to escort Caesar to the Capitol. He says he has great things planned.

Caesar bids the men to share some wine with him before they leave for the Capitol. Brutus hangs back, pondering the plot.

Good friends, go in, and taste some wine with me...

And we, like friends, will straight away go together.

That every like is not the same, O Caesar, the heart of Brutus yearns to think upon![5]

1. for thy humor: so you won't worry.   2. let me know some cause: tell me why.
3. I did yield to them: I let them affect my decision.   4. remember you: praise you to the senate.
5. That every . . . think upon: I am sorry to think that we may not be quite the friends that you believe.

THE LAST CHANCE

But Caesar still has allies...

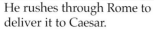
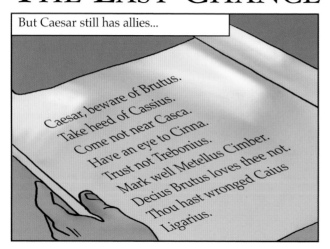

Caesar, beware of Brutus.
Take heed of Cassius.
Come not near Casca.
Have an eye to Cinna.
Trust not Trebonius.
Mark well Metellus Cimber.
Decius Brutus loves thee not.
Thou hast wronged Caius
Ligarius.

Artemidorus has written a letter to Caesar, warning him of the plot.

There is but one mind in all these men, and it is bent against Caesar.

If thou be'st not immortal, look about you: security gives way to conspiracy.

The mighty gods defend thee!

He rushes through Rome to deliver it to Caesar.

Meanwhile...

Bring me word, boy, if thy lord look well, for he went sickly forth.

Brutus's wife, Portia, is worried about her husband. She sends the slave Lucius to check on him.

Thou hast some suit[1] to Caesar, hast thou not?

That I have, lady. If it will please Caesar to be so good to Caesar as to hear me...

...I shall beseech him to befriend himself.[2]

The soothsayer rushes around the corner.

Why, know'st thou any harm's intended towards him?

None that I know will be, much that I fear may chance.

The soothsayer sees the crowd approaching and rushes to join it. He cannot give Portia a straight answer.

1. suit: request.   2. beseech him to befriend himself: urge him to look after his own interests.

Portia fears the plot will be discovered.

Caesar makes his way down the narrow streets. Artemidorus chases after the crowd with his letter.

Caesar sees the soothsayer who earlier predicted bad fortune on the Ides of March.

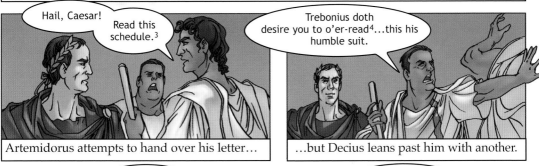

Artemidorus attempts to hand over his letter…

…but Decius leans past him with another.

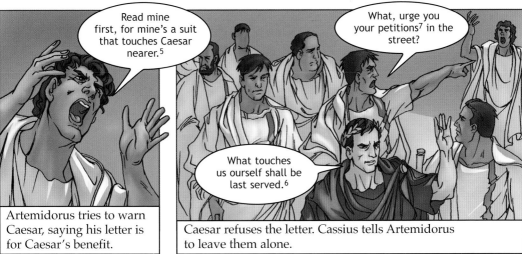

Artemidorus tries to warn Caesar, saying his letter is for Caesar's benefit.

Caesar refuses the letter. Cassius tells Artemidorus to leave them alone.

1. speed: favor.   2. enterprise: plan.   3. schedule: request.   4. o'er-read: read over.   5. touches Caesar nearer: affects Caesar more closely.   6. What touches . . . served: I'll deal with things that affect me last of all. (Caesar means he'll look after the affairs of the people as his first priority.)   7. petitions: requests.

Murder in the Senate

The senators of Rome make their way to the Senate House.

What is now amiss that Caesar and his Senate must redress?[2]

Trebonius knows his time,[1] for...he draws Mark Antony out of the way.

As the senators gather inside, Cassius and Brutus are nervous. Trebonius leads Mark Antony outside.

Caesar starts the session.

Thy brother by decree[3] is banished.

If thou dost bend, and pray, and fawn[4] for him...

...I spurn[5] thee like a cur[6] out of my way.

Is there no voice more worthy than my own, to sound more sweetly in great Caesar's ear?

Metellus Cimber kneels to ask for his brother's exile to be withdrawn.

Metellus asks if any other person will plead for his brother.

I kiss thy hand, but not in flattery, Caesar.

Desiring thee that[7] Publius Cimber may have an immediate freedom of repeal.[8]

Brutus comes forward and kisses Caesar's hand.

1. knows his time: acts on cue.   2. What is . . . redress?: What wrongs are there that we need to put right?
3. by decree: by the judgment of the courts.   4. fawn: beg.   5. spurn: kick.   6. cur: mongrel.
7. Desiring thee that: I want you to allow.   8. freedom of repeal: pardon.

Caesar cannot disguise his shock. He senses that Brutus is turning against him.

Cinna and Decius step up with the same request.

Caesar realizes that he is being surrounded.

Casca pulls a knife from inside his toga.

Casca stabs Caesar in the neck...

...and the others join in.

Finally, Brutus stabs his old friend as well.

The deed is done. The senators rejoice.

1. *Et tu, Brute?*: Latin for "Even you, Brutus?" (Caesar cannot believe his friend's betrayal).

MARK ANTONY: FRIEND OR FOE?

People and senators, be not affrighted[1]...

Fly not,[2] stand still. Ambition's debt is paid.[3]

Brutus reassures the shocked senators that the worst is over.

There is no harm intended to your person, nor to no Roman else.

So often shall the knot[4] of us be called the men that gave their country liberty.

A terrified old senator wonders if he'll be next. Mark Antony has run away to his house.

Let us bathe our hands in Caesar's blood up to the elbows.

Tell him, so please him come[6] unto this place...

...he shall be satisfied and, by my honor, depart untouched.

Mark Antony shall not love Caesar dead so well as Brutus living.[5]

I know that we shall have him well to friend.[7]

But yet have I a mind that fears him much.[8]

Mark Antony's servant says his master wishes to speak with them.

Brutus is confident, but Cassius is unsure.

1. affrighted: afraid.   2. Fly not: Don't run away.   3. Ambition's debt is paid: Caesar has paid the price for his ambition.   4. knot: group.   5. Mark Antony . . . living: Mark Antony will switch his loyalty to Brutus.   6. so please him come: let him come.   7. we shall . . . friend: he'll be a good ally.   8. yet have . . . much: I'm still wary of him.

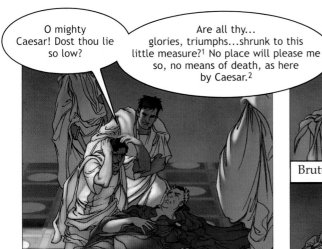

O mighty Caesar! Dost thou lie so low?

Are all thy... glories, triumphs...shrunk to this little measure?[1] No place will please me so, no means of death, as here by Caesar.[2]

To you our swords have leaden points,[3] Mark Antony.

Brutus says they mean him no harm.

Only be patient till we have appeased the multitude.[4]

Mark Antony kneels in horror before the body of his dead friend. If they plan to kill him too, he will die gladly.

He asks Mark Antony to wait until everything has been explained to the people.

Let each man render[5] me his bloody hand.

Mark Antony pretends to go along with the plan, and shakes each of the murderers' hands.

He tells them he will display Caesar's corpse to the outside world, and explain their actions to the people of Rome...

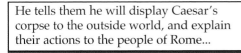

And in the pulpit, as becomes a friend,[6] speak in the order[7] of his funeral.

Thou art the ruins of the noblest man that ever lived in the tide of times.

...but secretly he has another plan.

After the others have left, Antony is alone with the body. He praises Caesar and swears revenge.

1. shrunk . . . measure: reduced to this (a dead body).   2. No place . . . by Caesar: I would be happiest to die now, alongside Caesar.   3. leaden points: blunt points, like a practice sword.   4. appeased the multitude: calmed the ordinary citizens.   5. render: offer.   6. as becomes a friend: as a friend should.   7. order: ritual.

SPEECHES TO THE PEOPLE

Meanwhile...

We will be satisfied! Let us be satisfied!

As Brutus and Cassius make their way into the forum,[1] the citizens swarm around them, demanding to know what has happened.

If then that friend demand[2] why Brutus rose against Caesar, this is my answer: Not that I loved Caesar less, but that I loved Rome more.

Here comes his body, mourned by Mark Antony.

Mark Antony carries Caesar's body toward the rostrum.

Climbing onto a rostrum,[3] Brutus argues that Caesar was killed for the sake of Rome.

With this I depart.[4] That, as I slew my best lover[5] for the good of Rome, I have the same dagger for myself...

...when it shall please my country to need my death.[6]

Live, Brutus! Live, live!

Brutus asks if he should kill himself too. The people are won over, and tell him not to.

I do entreat[7] you, not a man depart, save I alone,[8] till Antony have spoke.

He asks them all not to flatter him, and to stay to listen to Mark Antony's speech.

Friends, Romans, countrymen, lend me your ears.

I come to bury Caesar, not to praise him.

Mark Antony plans to turn the crowd against Brutus and the other assassins.

---

1. forum: a large, open, meeting place.   2. If then that friend demand: If someone asks.   3. rostrum: a raised platform.
4. depart: finish my speech.   5. lover: cherished friend.   6. when it . . . death: when the people of my country want me to die.   7. entreat: ask politely.   8. save I alone: except me.

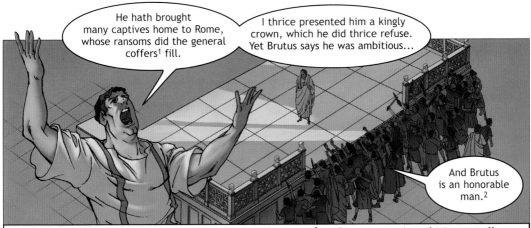

He then surprises everyone by praising Caesar. He says that Caesar wasn't ambitious at all. Everything Caesar did was for the good of Rome, not for himself.

He sheds tears on the rostrum, scorning Caesar's murderers.

O judgment, thou art fled to brutish beasts...

...and men have lost their reason!

But here's a parchment with the seal[3] of Caesar...'tis his will.[4]

If you have tears, prepare to shed them now.

We'll mutiny!

We'll burn the house of Brutus!

He reads them Caesar's will, which leaves a sum of money and the public parks to the people of Rome.

Go, fetch fire!

He tells them to light a funeral pyre for Caesar.

He points to the wounds made by the killers, enraging the crowd.

See what a rent[5] the envious Casca made. Through this the well-beloved Brutus stabbed.

Mischief, thou art afoot.[6]

Brutus and Cassius are rid[7] like madmen...

...through the gates of Rome.

A servant tells him that Caesar's nephew Octavius has arrived. Brutus and Cassius have escaped.

1. general coffers: state funds.   2. And Brutus is an honorable man: Mark Antony uses irony to cast doubt on Brutus' motives.   3. seal: a mark made in wax, used to show a document was genuine.
4. will: a legal document giving instructions for disposing of a dead person's property.   5. rent: wound.
6. afoot: underway.   7. are rid: have ridden.

REVENGE

Cinna the poet is walking along a nearby street.

He has a bad feeling because of a dream he had.

Suddenly a crowd of citizens come around the corner carrying torches and makeshift weapons.

I dreamt tonight that I did feast with Caesar...

...and things unluckily charge my fantasy.[1]

What is your name?

Where do you dwell?

Whither[2] are you going?

They surround Cinna, jostling him and asking questions.

Directly, I am going to Caesar's funeral.

I dwell by the Capitol...

Truly, my name is Cinna.

Tear him to pieces! He's a conspirator.

I am not Cinna the conspirator!

Tear him for his bad verses!

They mistake him for the Cinna who conspired against Caesar.

1. things unluckily charge my fantasy: events make me worry that I might end up dead too.
2. Whither: Where.

Mad for blood, the mob kills Cinna.

To Brutus's, to Cassius's!

Burn all!

He shall not live.

Look, with a spot I damn him.

Your brother too must die. Consent you,[1] Lepidus?

I do consent.

Mark Antony, Octavius, and Lepidus meet to look over the names of Caesar's murderers, which include Lepidus's brother...

...and Mark Antony's nephew.

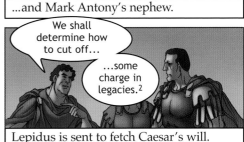

We shall determine how to cut off...

...some charge in legacies.[2]

Lepidus is sent to fetch Caesar's will.

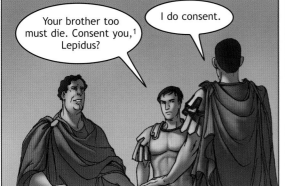

This is a slight unmeritable[3] man, meet to be sent on errands.[4]

Mark Antony doesn't think Lepidus deserves a part in their triumvirate[5]...

Then take we down his load and turn him off...

...like to the empty ass.[6]

...but he will be good for simple tasks for as long as he is needed.

Therefore let our alliance be combined...

Our best friends made, our means stretched.[7]

Octavius and Mark Antony plan to gather allies for an attack on Brutus and Cassius.

1. Consent you?: Do you agree?   2. We shall . . . legacies: We'll work out a plan to save some of the money that was promised to the people.   3. unmeritable: unworthy.   4. meet to be sent on errands: fit to be sent to perform minor tasks.
5. triumvirate: a leadership team of three people.   6. Then take we . . . empty ass: Then we send him away like a useless donkey.   7. our means stretched: our power combined.

UNEASY ALLIES

Several months later...

Brutus has amassed his forces in Sardis,[1] ready to face the armies of Octavius and Mark Antony. Since leaving Rome, Brutus and Cassius have grown cautious of each other.

I do not doubt but that my noble master will appear such as he is, full of regard and honor.[2]

A soldier brings the news that Cassius will soon arrive.

Thou hast described a hot friend cooling.

Cassius and his army arrive.

Stand, ho! Speak the word along.[3]

Stand.

Stand.

Let us not wrangle.[4]

Bid them move away.[5]

Brutus refuses to argue before his troops.

You yourself are much condemned to have an itching palm.[6]

You know that you are Brutus that speak this, or, by the gods, this speech were else your last.[7]

Cassius is angry with Brutus for prosecuting his friend, the governor of Sardis, for taking bribes. Brutus points out that Cassius himself is known to take bribes.

1. Sardis: a city now known as Sart, located in the west of Turkey.   2. I do not doubt . . . honor: I have no doubt that Cassius will be here soon, eager to join you again.   3. Speak the word along: Pass the order to stand along the line. 4. wrangle: argue.   5. Bid them move away: Ask the soldiers to go away.   6. condemned . . . palm: accused of being greedy.   7. You know . . . else your last: If you weren't Brutus, I'd kill you for saying this.

The pair exchange insults. Brutus believes that they killed Caesar to make Rome better, and that Cassius's dishonesty makes a mockery of this aim.

Away, slight man!

Urge me no more,[1] I shall forget myself.

You love me not.

I do not like your faults.

Come, Antony and young Octavius, come.

Revenge yourselves alone on Cassius.[2]

Ashamed by his brother-in-law's criticism, Cassius pulls out his dagger to kill himself.

Sheathe your dagger.

Give me your hand.

And my heart too.

Brutus grabs Cassius's hand to stop him from harming himself. The argument is over.

Portia is dead.

Brutus is upset because his wife, Portia, became grief-stricken in his absence. She sent her servants away and killed herself in a house fire.

With this she fell distract and, her attendants absent, swallowed fire.[3]

Now sit we close about this taper here.

A messenger, Messala, arrives from Rome.

Messala says that Octavius and Mark Antony have put to death a hundred senators, including Cicero.

---

1. Urge me no more: Stop provoking me.   2. Revenge yourselves alone on Cassius: Cassius wants to take the punishment for murdering Caesar by taking his own life.   3. swallowed fire: suffocated on the smoke from the fire.

THE GHOST OF CAESAR

Messala tells the generals that Octavius and Mark Antony have marched to nearby Philippi.[1]

The battlefield is sparse and desolate.

'Tis better that the enemy seek us, so shall he waste his means,[2] weary his soldiers.

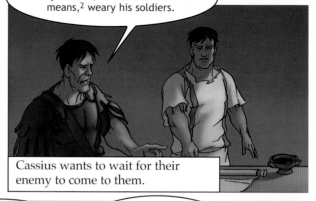

Cassius wants to wait for their enemy to come to them.

The people 'twixt[3] Philippi and this ground do stand but in a forced affection.[4]

Then, with your will,[5] go on. We'll along[6] ourselves, and meet them at Philippi.

Canst thou hold up thy heavy eyes awhile, and touch thy instrument a strain or two?[7]

However, Brutus believes it is best to head to Philippi first. Cassius concedes to his brother-in-law, and says good night.

Brutus calls for his trusted soldiers to keep him company.

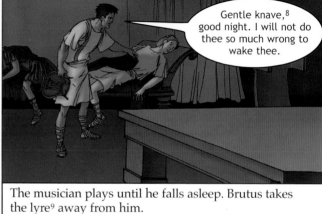

Gentle knave,[8] good night. I will not do thee so much wrong to wake thee.

The music calms Brutus's thoughts.

The musician plays until he falls asleep. Brutus takes the lyre[9] away from him.

1. Philippi: a place in present-day northern Greece.   2. waste his means: use up his supplies.   3. 'twixt: between.
4. do stand . . . affection: are allies only because they fear us (Brutus is worried they will go over to Mark Antony's side).
5. with your will: as you wish.   6. along: march.   7. touch thy . . . two: play a little music on your instrument.
8. knave: soldier, knight.   9. lyre: a stringed musical instrument.

28

Brutus opens a scroll and begins to read at the desk by candlelight.

Let me see, let me see. Is not the leaf[1] turned down where I left[2] reading?

How ill[3] this taper burns! Who comes here?

He glimpses a shadow...

Art thou some god, some angel, or some devil...

...that makest my blood cold and my hair to stare?[4]

...and is terrified by the shape that appears before him.

Why comest thou?

To tell thee thou shalt see me at Philippi.

The ghost of Caesar stands in the tent doorway.

Now I have taken heart,[5] thou vanishest.

The ghost vanishes, leaving the tent door flapping in the wind.

Boy! Lucius! Varro! Claudius!

Sirs, awake!

Brutus quickly wakes the others.

Go and commend me[6] to my brother Cassius.

Bid him set on his powers betimes before[7] and we will follow.

Didst thou see any thing?

Nor I, my lord.

No, my lord, I saw nothing.

Nothing, my lord.

Brutus orders the soldiers to go to Cassius and stir his troops. It's time to march.

1. leaf: page. (Shakespeare forgets that Roman books were scrolls, and did not have pages.)   2. left: stopped.
3. ill: badly.   4. stare: stand on end.   5. taken heart: recovered my courage.
6. commend me: pass on my greetings.   7. Bid him . . . before: Ask him to ready his troops as soon as possible.

PREPARING FOR BATTLE

On the plains at Philippi the two armies ready themselves for battle: on one side, Octavius and Mark Antony...

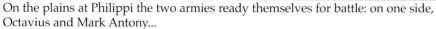

...on the other, Brutus and Cassius.

> Octavius, lead your battle softly on,[1] upon the left hand of the even field.

Mark Antony and Octavius discuss tactics.

> Words before blows: is it so, countrymen?

> Good words are better than bad strokes, Octavius.

> In your bad strokes, Brutus, you give good words.

> Not that we love words better, as you do.

> Witness the hole you made in Caesar's heart, crying, "Long live! Hail, Caesar!"[2]

The leaders ride out onto the battlefield.

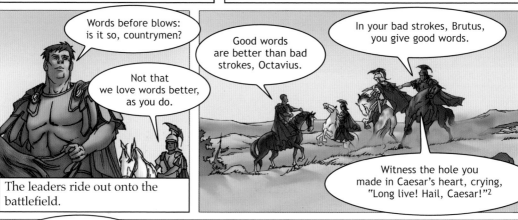

> I draw a sword against conspirators. When think you that the sword goes up[3] again?

> ...or till another Caesar have added slaughter to the sword of traitors.[5]

> Never, till Caesar's three and thirty[4] wounds be well avenged...

Octavius runs out of patience.

1. lead your battle softly on: advance your army with caution.   2. In your . . . "Hail Caesar!": Mark Antony is saying that Brutus is dishonest, because he praised Caesar ("good words") after murdering him ("bad strokes"). 3. goes up: will be put back in its sheath.   4. three and thirty: Caesar was stabbed thirty-three times. 5. till another . . . traitors: until he (Octavius Caesar) has been killed as well.

Thou canst not die by traitors' hands unless thou bring'st them with thee.[1]

I was not born to die on Brutus's sword.

A peevish[2] schoolboy, worthless of such honor.

Old Cassius still!

Come, Antony, away! Defiance, traitors, hurl we in your teeth.

If you dare fight today, come to the field. If not, when you have stomachs.[3]

Octavius makes his way back to his army.

Cassius speaks to the messenger Messala.

What says my General?

He tells of an omen he witnessed.

Two mighty eagles fell...

...and there they perched.

This morning are they fled away and gone...

And in their steads[4] do ravens, crows, and kites[5] fly o'er our heads.

If we do lose this battle, then is this the very last time we shall speak together. What are you then determined to do?

Brutus comes back to Cassius's side.

Think not, thou noble Roman, that ever Brutus will go bound[6] to Rome. He bears too great a mind.[7]

Brutus says that even though suicide is the traditional custom in defeat, it is cowardly. Cassius asks if he will let himself be captured in that case. Brutus says he will not.

1. unless . . . thee: unless there are traitors in your own army.   2. peevish: silly, moody.   3. when you have stomachs: when you are brave enough.   4. in their steads: in place of them.   5. ravens, crows, and kites: birds that are bad omens before a battle, as they are scavengers.   6. bound: chained like a prisoner.   7. bears too great a mind: is too noble-minded to submit to imprisonment.

31

THE CHAOS OF BATTLE

On the plains of Philippi, the two sides meet in battle …

Let them set on[1] at once. For I perceive but cold demeanor[2] in Octavius's wing, and sudden push gives them the overthrow.[3]

Ride, ride, Messala. Let them all come down.

Brutus gives Messala orders to tell what's left of his troops to attack Octavius's forces.

Meanwhile, Cassius's troops have fled.

The villains fly![4] Myself have to mine own turned enemy.[5]

This ensign[6] here of mine was turning back…

I slew[7] the coward, and did take it from him.

Cassius saw his own standard-bearer fleeing, and killed him.

32   1. set on: attack.   2. cold demeanor: lack of spirit for the fight.   3. gives them the overthrow: will overthrow them.
4. fly: run away.   5. Myself have . . . enemy: My men are deserting me.   6. ensign: standard-bearer. He carried the eagle emblem which Roman soldiers followed into battle.   7. slew: killed.

Brutus...who,
having some advantage
on Octavius, took it
too eagerly.

His soldiers
fell to spoil,[1] whilst
we by Antony are all
enclosed.[2]

Titinius, an officer in
Cassius's army, says that
Brutus sent his men in too
early. Now they are looting
instead of fighting.

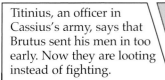

Fly further off, my
lord... Mark Antony is in
your tents, my lord.

Cassius's slave, Pindarus, urges
him to retreat.

Mark Antony's troops are destroying Cassius's camp,
setting fire to the tents and killing the servants.

Soon Pindarus reports that Titinius has been
captured. He was seen surrounded by
soldiers. Cassius is overwhelmed with grief.

Now be a freeman,
and with this good sword, that
ran through Caesar's bowels,
search this bosom.[3]

Cassius hands his sword to Pindarus. He will
give him his freedom if he'll carry out one final
task—to kill his master.

O, coward that
I am, to live so long to
see my best friend taken
before my face!

Far from this country
Pindarus shall run, where never
Roman shall take note of[4] him.

Pindarus obeys. He kills Cassius and rides off.

1. having some . . . fell to spoil: while the soldiers had the upper hand, they started looting.   2. enclosed: surrounded.
3. search this bosom: stab me in the chest.   4. take note of: notice.

The Shame of Defeat

But Titinius isn't dead...

Pindarus thought he saw him captured by the enemy, but he was actually riding with allies.

It is but change, Titinius...

...for Octavius is overthrown by noble Brutus's power, as Cassius's legions are by Antony.

Titinius approaches with Messala, who says that the outcome is uncertain.

These tidings would well comfort Cassius.[1]

He lies not like the living.

O my heart!

He catches sight of Cassius's body on the ground.

Messala goes to find Brutus. Meanwhile, overcome with grief, Titinius takes Cassius's sword...

By your leave, gods: this is a Roman's part[2]...

O setting sun, as in thy red rays thou dost sink to night...

...so in his red blood Cassius's day is set, the sun of Rome is set! Where art thou, Pindarus!

...and kills himself as well.

Come, Cassius's sword, and find Titinius's heart.

1. These tidings . . . Cassius: Although Cassius's forces are losing, he'll be glad that Brutus's are doing better.
2. this is a Roman's part: this (suicide) is a fitting way for a Roman to behave.

Where, where, Messala, doth his body lie?

Lo, yonder, and Titinius mourning it.

A crowd of other soldiers arrive, including Messala and Brutus.

Seeing that Titinius is dead, Brutus remembers Caesar's ghost appearing to him.

Titinius's face is upward.

O Julius Caesar, thou art mighty yet![1]

Thy spirit walks abroad,[2] and turns our swords in our own proper entrails.[3]

He can see that the battle is almost lost…

…but he rouses his men for one final fight.

'Tis three o'clock, and, Romans, yet ere night[4] we shall try fortune[5] in a second fight.

Lucilius, come. And come, young Cato. Let us to the field.

Labeo and Flavius, set our battles on.

The remaining forces rush into battle.

---

1. yet: still.   2. abroad: away from its proper place, in the underworld.   3. in our own proper entrails: into our own stomachs.   4. yet ere night: before nightfall.   5. try fortune: try our luck.

THE FINAL THROW OF THE DICE

Brutus leads his men forward.

Yet, countrymen, o, yet hold up your heads!

He and Cato see Mark Antony's forces waiting.

Who will go with me? I will proclaim my name about the field.

I am the son of Marcus Cato, ho!

Cato and Lucilius ride to the enemy.

Cato throws himself into the shield wall...

...and meets his death.

O young and noble Cato, art thou down?[1]

Why, now thou diest as bravely as Titinius.

I am Brutus, Marcus Brutus, I...

There is so much that thou wilt kill me straight.[2]

Enemy soldiers surround Lucilius. Pretending to be Brutus, he offers the soldiers money to kill him.

1. art thou down?: are you dead?   2. There is . . . straight: Here's enough money to pay you to kill me immediately.

We must not. A noble prisoner!

Room, ho! Tell Antony, Brutus is ta'en.[1]

But the soldiers don't want to kill such an important prisoner.

Where is he?

Mark Antony asks to see Brutus.

Lucilius reveals his true identity, and declares that Brutus would never allow himself to be captured.

Safe, Antony. Brutus is safe enough.

I dare assure thee that no enemy shall ever take alive the noble Brutus.

This is not Brutus, friend, but, I assure you, a prize no less in worth.

Keep this man safe, give him all kindness. I had rather have such men my friends than enemies.

Mark Antony is not angry that it isn't Brutus. He admires Lucilius's sacrifice.

Mark Antony returns to his tent, and gives orders to find the real Brutus.

Go on, and see whether Brutus be alive or dead.

And bring us word unto Octavius's tent...

...how everything is chanced.[2]

1. ta'en: taken, captured. 2. how everything is chanced: what has happened.

THE DEATH OF A NOBLE ROMAN

At the edge of the battlefield, Brutus regroups his remaining men.

Come, poor remains of friends, rest on this rock.

Brutus whispers something into Clitus's ear.

What, I, my lord? No, not for all the world.

Shall I do such a deed?

Next he whispers to Dardanius.

Clitus asks Dardanius what Brutus wanted.

What ill[1] request did Brutus make to thee?

To kill him, Clitus. Look, he meditates.[2]

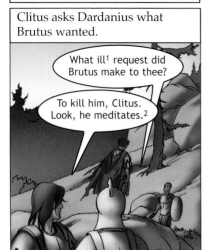

The ghost of Caesar hath appeared to me two several[3] times by night...

...at Sardis once, and this last night here in Philippi fields.

I know my hour is come.

Not so, my lord.

Brutus now addresses Volumnius.

I prithee,[4] hold thou my sword-hilts, whilst I run on it.

1. ill: awful, terrible.   2. meditates: thinks deeply.   3, several: separate.   4. I prithee: I beg you.

Fly, fly, my lord! There is no tarrying[1] here.

Hence! I will follow.

Clitus warns that the enemy is closing in. Brutus says he'll escape with them . . .

I prithee, Strato, stay thou by thy lord. Thou art a fellow of a good respect.[2]

. . . but he does not intend to run.

Hold, then, my sword, and turn away thy face, while I do run upon it.

Give me your hand first. Fare you well, my lord.

Caesar, now be still. I killed not thee with half so good a will.[3]

Brutus looks to the heavens.

He pulls himself onto the sword, and dies.

Octavius appears, with Messala and Lucilius as his captives.

This was the noblest Roman of them all.

All the conspirators, save only he, did that they did in envy of great Caesar.[6]

He only, in a general honest thought and common good to all, made one of them.

Free from the bondage[4] you are in, Messala. The conquerors can but make a fire of him.[5]

Messala asks Strato what has happened to Brutus.

The battle is won. Mark Antony pays tribute to Brutus. Even though he was one of Caesar's killers, he alone had honorable motives.

1. tarrying: delaying.   2. respect: reputation.   3. I killed . . . a will: I found it harder to kill you than I find it to kill myself.   4. bondage: the prison of life.
5. can but . . . fire of him: can only place him on a funeral pyre.   6. All the . . . Caesar: All the other conspirators, aside from Brutus, killed Caesar through envy.

THE END

William Shakespeare was born in Stratford-upon-Avon, Warwickshire, England, in 1564, possibly on April 23rd, which is St. George's Day—the feast-day of England's patron saint. His father was a respected businessman who became mayor of Stratford, though it seems he never learned to write. We know nothing of William's childhood and education, except that he did not go to college. He probably learned Latin at the King's New School in Stratford.

In 1582 he married Anne Hathaway. He was only 18; she was 26, and pregnant. Their daughter Susanna was born 6 months later, and in 1585 they had twins, Hamnet and Judith. Anne and the children seem to have stayed in Stratford all their lives, even while William was living and working in London.

The Chandos Portrait of Shakespeare, *by Joseph Taylor, c. 1610, once owned by the Duke of Chandos.*

LONDON AND THE THEATER

Shakespeare was acting and writing plays in London by about 1590. We do not know how he made his living before that, or how he got started as a playwright. London in the 1590s was an exciting place for anyone interested in the stage. Theaters—or "playhouses"— were not allowed in the city of London itself; they were built on the north side of London, outside the city walls, and in Southwark, on the south bank of the Thames. Many playwrights were active in London at this time. Christopher Marlowe wrote several blockbuster tragedies before being killed in a brawl at the age of 29. Other well-known writers included Thomas Dekker, Thomas Kyd, John Webster, Thomas Middleton, and the partnership of Francis Beaumont and John Fletcher. In the 1600s, Ben Jonson wrote a series of clever and witty comedies; Shakespeare acted in some of them.

Writing plays was not an especially well-paid job—the author's fee might be less than the value of an actor's costume. But Shakespeare was a keen businessman. In 1594 he became a shareholder in a new acting company, the Lord Chamberlain's Men. This meant that he invested money in the company, and in return he was paid a share of the profits made by the company. With the money he made, he was able to buy land in Stratford for his family, and a magnificent house, New Place. He also became a shareholder in the new Globe Theatre, which opened in 1599.

The Classical World

William Shakespeare returned several times to the ancient world of Greece and Rome in his plays, especially the tragedies. Among his most famous are *Julius Caesar* and *Antony and Cleopatra*, though he also wrote *Coriolanus*, about a proud Roman general; *Timon of Athens*, about an Athenian nobleman who comes to hate the world; *Troilus and Cressida*, about the legendary Trojan War; and *Titus Andronicus*, a bloody revenge play about a fictional Roman. One of Shakespeare's comedies, *Pericles*, concerns a prince of Tyre (in modern Lebanon).

There's no evidence that Shakespeare ever traveled abroad, and some scholars argue that he couldn't even read Latin or Greek. He would, however, have been able to read translations of ancient works, and could base his plays on these.

Other Plays by WILLIAM SHAKESPEARE

Note: We do not know the exact dates of most of Shakespeare's plays, or even the exact order in which they were written. The dates shown here are only approximate.

1590:	*Henry VI, Part I*	1602:	*Twelfth Night*
1591:	*Henry VI, Part II*	1603:	*All's Well That Ends Well*
	Henry VI, Part III	1604:	*Othello*
1593:	*Richard III*		*Measure for Measure*
1594:	*Edward III**	1605:	*King Lear*
	Titus Andronicus	1606:	*Macbeth*
	The Comedy of Errors	1608:	*Pericles*
	The Taming of the Shrew		*Coriolanus*
	The Two Gentlemen of Verona		*Timon of Athens*
1595:	*Love's Labour's Lost*		*Troilus and Cressida*
	Richard II		*Antony and Cleopatra*
1596:	*King John*	1610:	*Cymbeline*
	Romeo and Juliet	1611:	*The Winter's Tale*
	A Midsummer Night's Dream		*The Tempest*
1597:	*The Merchant of Venice*	1613:	*Henry VIII***
	The Merry Wives of Windsor	1614:	*The Two Noble Kinsmen***
	Henry IV, Part I		
1598:	*Henry IV, Part II*		
1599:	*Much Ado About Nothing*		
	As You Like It		
	Julius Caesar		
	Henry V		
	Hamlet		

*May not be by Shakespeare
**By Shakespeare and John Fletcher

Shakespeare probably wrote two other plays, *Love's Labour's Won* and *Cardenio*, which have not survived.

Gaius Julius Caesar was born in 100 B.C. into a powerful political family. Like other young men who wished to become politicians, he had to progress through a series of jobs called the *cursus honorum* ("the course of honors"). Rome was a republic at the time, meaning that it was not governed by a single man, but by a large assembly of wealthy men from powerful families. This assembly was called the senate.

Caesar spent a year as governor of Spain, which was then a Roman province. On returning to Rome, he created what is known as the First Triumvirate, a partnership with his allies Pompey and Crassus. ("Triumvirate" means "a group of three men.") With their help, Caesar was elected to the consulship, the highest level of office, in 59 B.C.

An 18th-century bust of Julius Caesar.

AMBITION AND SUCCESS

Caesar was ambitious, and he left Rome the following year to take on the governorship of Gaul, at that time an enormous region covering modern-day France, Belgium, the Netherlands, Switzerland, Northern Italy, and some of Germany. After eight years, Caesar finally conquered the Gaulish tribes.

He was thought a hero by the people of Rome, but the senate was worried. Many felt that Caesar's triumphs made him dangerous. He commanded a huge and loyal army. Pompey, Caesar's former ally, turned against him, and ordered him to return to Rome, leaving his army behind.

Caesar obeyed the demand that he return, but did not disband his forces. Instead, he marched his army back to Rome, crossing the Rubicon River with one of his legions. The crossing of this river was an act forbidden by Roman law and it sparked a civil war between the senate and Caesar.

CAESAR AND POMPEY

Realizing Caesar had many supporters in Rome, Pompey fled with a group of loyal senators to Brundisium (now Brindisi) in the south of Italy.

After Caesar had defeated Pompey's supporters in Spain and Greece, Pompey fled to Alexandria in Egypt, which at that time was ruled by Rome but kept its own royal family, the Ptolemies. Before Caesar could face Pompey in battle again, Pompey was assassinated by a Roman officer. His head was presented to Caesar, who is said to have wept when he saw it. After this, Caesar became involved in the conflict between King Ptolemy XIII of Egypt and the king's sister, Cleopatra. Caesar sided with Cleopatra and overthrew Ptolemy.

Afterwards, despite having a wife, Calpurnia, in Rome, Caesar had a relationship with Cleopatra, and she bore him a son, Caesarion.

CAESAR THE DICTATOR

Over the coming years, Caesar continued to have military successes in the East, sweeping through Asia Minor (now Turkey) to quell the disturbances there. Caesar was effectively a dictator (absolute ruler) in Rome, and the senate did his bidding. In 45 B.C., he named his nephew Octavian (called Octavius in Shakespeare's play) as heir to his wealth and to the leadership of Rome.

Distrust of Caesar's power led a group of senators to plot his death. Though they committed their crime with the intention of restoring the Republic, it had the opposite effect, tearing Rome apart and heralding the beginnings of the Empire under Octavian.

Caesar's character has been a source of controversy to historians and scholars alike. Some see him as a noble man, who cared for the people of Rome. Others judge him a ruthless and ambitious politician, who wanted to cling on to power at any cost.

He was known to suffer from fits, which some modern scholars believe were signs of epilepsy, and he was a writer of some talent, penning long accounts of his campaign against the Gauls. Certainly he was a brilliant military commander, and his life was a turning point in Roman history.

ANCIENT WRITINGS

• **Suetonius** (c.69–c.130 A.D.) wrote biographies of twelve Roman leaders under the title *De Vita Caesarum* (*About the Lives of the Caesars*), of which Julius Caesar was the first.

• **Cassius Dio** (c.155–c.229) was the son of a senator and published a history of Rome in 80 volumes. Books 37–44 deal with Julius Caesar's time.

• **Plutarch** (c.46–120) was a Greek historian and biographer who wrote a series of books called *Parallel Lives*, each of which compared the lives of a famous Greek and a famous Roman. As part of this series, he wrote about both Julius Caesar and Mark Antony.

• **Appian** (c.95–c.165) was a Greek historian born in Alexandria. He wrote a history of Rome in 24 volumes. Five of these books deal with the end of the Roman Republic.

• And, of course, there is **Julius Caesar** himself. Much of his work is lost, but two historical pieces in particular are useful to students of history. *Commentarii de Bello Gallico* (*Account of the War in Gaul*) tells Caesar's version of his conquests in Gaul; and *Commentarii de Bello Civili* (*Account of the Civil War*) is about his war with Pompey after Caesar had crossed the Rubicon.

According to legend, the city of Rome was founded in 753 B.C. by twin brothers, Romulus and Remus, sons of the god Mars. They later quarreled and Romulus killed his brother, naming the city after himself.

In truth, archeological evidence suggests that the city grew from small farming communities on the fertile banks of the Tiber River.

Because the Gauls destroyed all of Rome's historical records when they ravaged the city in 390 B.C., we can't be too certain about how Rome worked as a kingdom. However, we know that Rome was ruled by a succession of kings, who were aided by the senate, a group of wealthy aristocrats who helped the king make decisions for the city.

THE ROMAN REPUBLIC

The Roman Republic began in 510 B.C. when the king Tarquinius Superbus was expelled from Rome after a reign of violence and destruction. Interestingly, it was Marcus Junius Brutus's ancestor Lucius who put forward the motion to end the monarchy. Once the back of this vicious tyrant was seen, the role of king was replaced by that of consul.

The consulate was initially formed of two people, but, over time, new levels of office were created to both lighten the responsibility of the consul and to avoid the possibility of another tyrant. Beneath the consul were the praetors, who had power in the law courts. Next came the censors, who conducted the census, an event in which the population was counted and examined. Tribunes were elected by the common

people of Rome (known as plebeians). As representatives of the massive population of Rome, they held great power in the senate. They were able to interject if they did not agree with a decision being made in the senate.

The transition from republic to imperial rule was quite speedy. At the time of Caesar's assassination, Rome was the capital of a world empire. Mark Antony, Octavian, and Marcus Lepidus soon formed what is known as the Second Triumvirate. While Mark Antony was in Alexandria, Octavian turned the people of Rome against him. This was the start of several civil wars that would eventually bring the Roman Republic to an end.

THE ROMAN EMPIRE

The senate granted Octavian the title Augustus (Latin for "majestic") in 27 B.C., and over the next forty years he set the standard for all following emperors. As the first sole ruler of Rome after the republic, he is known as the first emperor. After expanding into Greece and the Middle East, the empire became very large, and difficult to rule from a central location.

Under Emperor Constantine I, the Empire split into two, east and west, and the center shifted to Constantinople (modern-day Istanbul in Turkey); Rome was no longer as important.

Toward the end of the fourth century A.D., Christianity became the official religion of the Empire, and the Romans abandoned their worship of other gods and goddesses. Other nations began to have more success in battle against the Roman Empire: first the Gauls, in 390,

The Roman Colosseum could seat 45,000 people, each of whom would have passed through one of the 80 available entrances. They came to watch gladiatorial matches, plays, and sometimes mock sea battles.

penetrated deep into Rome; and then in 410, the Visigoths took control of the city. Both times the Romans were forced to pay the attacking armies to retreat.

ART AND THEATER IN ROME

Art forms of many kinds flourished in Ancient Rome. Poets recited their works, sculptors carved statues, painters decorated the walls of houses and public buildings. Architects built temples and monuments to glorify Roman triumphs and their gods. Evidence of this culture still exists today in museums, in Rome itself, and throughout the former empire.

Romans loved a spectacle, whether in the law courts, where cases were heard; in the grand Colosseum, where gladiatorial competitions were held; or in the open-air theaters, where plays were shown.

Comedies were popular, and some of the works of playwrights such as Plautus and Terence can still be read today. Tragedies—plays about suffering and human folly—were also common, and these often followed the Greek example, with few actors and a chorus.

Theaters were semicircular in shape, with tiers of seats looking down onto the stage below. The seats were made of stone or wood, so spectators would often bring their own cushions to make the experience more comfortable.

1558
Elizabeth, daughter of Henry VIII, becomes Queen of England.

1564
William Shakespeare is born around April 23rd in Stratford-upon-Avon, Warwickshire.

1576
The Theatre, the first permanent playhouse in London, is built in Shoreditch, just outside the City of London.

1582
Shakespeare marries Anne Hathaway.

1583
Shakespeare's daughter Susanna is born.

1585
Birth of Shakespeare's twins: Hamnet and Judith.

1587
Mary, Queen of Scots, is executed after being implicated in a plot to murder Queen Elizabeth.

1592
An outbreak of plague closes the playhouses; instead of plays, Shakespeare writes poems and sonnets.

1594
The playhouses reopen. Shakespeare joins the Lord Chamberlain's Men as actor and playwright.

1596
Shakespeare's son Hamnet dies at age 11.

1597
Shakespeare buys New Place, the second-biggest house in Stratford.

1599
The Globe opens on Bankside. Shakespeare is a "sharer" or stockholder. He writes *Julius Caesar*.

1603
Queen Elizabeth dies without an heir. James VI of Scotland becomes king of England, taking the title King James I.

1605
The Gunpowder Plot, a conspiracy to assassinate James I and his Parliament, is foiled on November 5th.

1613
Shakespeare's Globe is destroyed by fire but rebuilt the following year.

1616
William Shakespeare dies in Stratford on April 23rd.

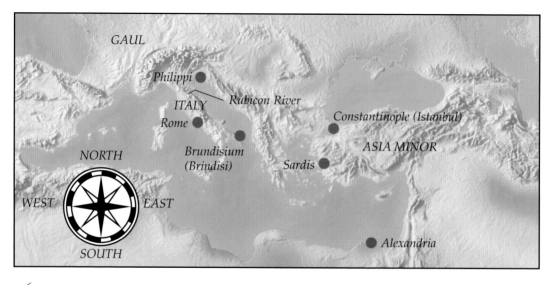

ADAPTATIONS OF *JULIUS CAESAR*

Julius Caesar, with its grand battle scenes, lends itself to very elaborate performances. In 1916, to commemorate the 300th anniversary of Shakespeare's death, an audience of 40,000 witnessed a performance in Beachwood Canyon, Hollywood. The students of two local high schools played opposing armies, and the battle scenes were performed on a huge stage as well as the surrounding hillsides.

At the Hollywood Bowl in 1962, a performance featured 300 gladiators, 300 captives of Caesar, and a total of 3,000 soldiers in the battle scenes. The enormous stage was dominated by a central tower 80 feet (24 m) in height.

CONSPIRACY

In 1864, famed Shakespearean actor John Wilkes Booth played Mark Antony in a benefit performance of *Julius Caesar* at the Winter Garden Theatre, New York. This landmark production raised funds to erect a statue of Shakespeare in Central Park, which remains to this day.

Incredibly, Booth was involved in his own conspiracy. Just six months later, he assassinated American president Abraham Lincoln in the presidential box of Ford's Theatre, Washington DC. Immediately after the murder, Booth is reported to have jumped down onto the stage, crying out *"sic semper tyrannis"* ("thus always to tyrants"). This Latin phrase is attributed to the real Marcus Junius Brutus at the time of Caesar's assassination. Strangely, Booth's father and brother, also Shakespearean actors, were both named Junius Brutus.

RECENT PRODUCTIONS

Like many of Shakespeare's plays, there have been numerous television and film adaptations of *Julius Caesar*. Marlon Brando won an Oscar for his role as Mark Antony in a 1953 film of the play, and Charlton Heston played Antony twice on film: once in 1950, then again in 1970.

Shakespeare's play continues to be staged to this day, and some of the greatest actors of each generation have taken on the roles. Brutus is seen to be the most interesting and challenging, and it is widely agreed that his is the central role, rather than Caesar's.

Mark Antony on the steps of the Capitol, as played by Marlon Brando in Joseph L. Mankiewicz's 1953 film Julius Caesar.

IF YOU ENJOYED THIS BOOK, YOU MIGHT LIKE TO TRY
THESE OTHER TITLES IN THE BARRON'S *GRAPHIC CLASSICS* SERIES:

Adventures of Huckleberry Finn Mark Twain

Dr. Jekyll and Mr. Hyde Robert Louis Stevenson

Dracula Bram Stoker

Frankenstein Mary Shelley

Hamlet William Shakespeare

The Hunchback of Notre Dame Victor Hugo

Jane Eyre Charlotte Brontë

Journey to the Center of the Earth Jules Verne

Kidnapped Robert Louis Stevenson

Macbeth William Shakespeare

The Man in the Iron Mask Alexandre Dumas

Moby Dick Herman Melville

Oliver Twist Charles Dickens

A Tale of Two Cities Charles Dickens

The Three Musketeers Alexandre Dumas

Treasure Island Robert Louis Stevenson

Wuthering Heights Emily Brontë